THE GIRL
WHO SAT BY
THE ASHES

THE GIRL
WHO SAT BY
THE ASHES

❀ ❀ ❀ ❀ ❀ ❀ ❀ ❀

by Padraic Colum
illustrated by Imero Gobbato

THE MACMILLAN COMPANY, NEW YORK
COLLIER-MACMILLAN LIMITED, LONDON

E8 | 320 |

398.4
C 72 gi

For
My Name Child
Colum Gavan-Duffy

❀ Contents

THE GIRL
WHO SAT BY
THE ASHES

THE COMING OF CROW-FEATHER CLOAK

I ❀ BECAUSE SHE USED TO HERD GOATS IN THE HIGH
places and the rocky places, she went by the
name of Girl-go-with-the-Goats. But that was not
the name that she herself called herself. She called
herself Maid-alone.

Her feet were scratched with briars and
bruised with stones. She was dressed in rags
threaded together. And neither the red of pleasure
nor the red of health had ever come into her face.

She lived with her stepmother, Dame Dale,
and her two stepsisters, Berry-bright and Buttercup.
Now one day as Berry-bright was dizening herself

with a necklace of beads and Buttercup was looking at herself in a plate of brass, an Old Woman came up to the house. Her dress was the queerest that anyone ever saw, a Cloak of Crow-feathers and nothing else.

"My, my, my," said the Old Woman as she came into the house. "My, my, my, what became of the big tree that used to grow fornenst your little house?"

"The big tree!" said Berry-bright. "I have heard my mother speak of that big tree. But she never saw it herself. They say that the gypsies once lighted their fires around that big tree, and that the leaves withered and the branches and the root, and the tree died away. But my mother never remembers to have seen it."

"My, my, my," said the Old Woman. "It must be a long time since I was round this way. And where is the well that used to be on my right-hand side as I came into the house?"

"I used to hear my grandmother speak of that well," said Buttercup. "But it was dried up before her time."

"My, my, my," said the Old Woman. "It's a

2

long time since I was round this way. But now that I'm here, maidens dear, put the griddle on the fire and knead and bake a cake for me."

"There's no fire on the hearthstone as you see," said Berry-bright, "and we are not going to put down a fire for you now."

"Nor can we knead a cake and put it on the griddle for you," said Buttercup.

"We have just washed our hands in new milk," said Berry-bright.

"As we wash them every day," said Buttercup.

"So that our hands will be as white as blossoms," said Berry-bright. "In three months from this the King's son is to choose out a maiden to wed."

"And there are no maidens fairer than we two," said Buttercup, "and one or the other of us the King's son is sure to marry."

"And so we have to keep our hands white and fair," said Berry-bright. "We couldn't think of putting down a fire now that we have washed them in new milk."

"And to put a griddle on!" said Buttercup.

4

"That would be to hold them over the fire and make the skin of our hands split."

"And to knead a cake!" said Berry-bright. "That would be to roughen our hands. The end of it is, Old Woman, we can't do anything for you."

"My, my, my," said the Old Woman. "Then I will get nothing to stay my hunger."

"If you had come before we washed our hands with new milk," said Buttercup, "we should have done what you'd ask."

Then they went on doing what they had been doing before, one looking at herself in a plate of brass and the other dizening herself with a necklace of beads. And the Old Woman in the Cloak of Crow-feathers was standing there looking at them when Girl-go-with-the-Goats came in.

"Did you milk the goats?" said Berry-bright.

"I did," said Girl-go-with-the-Goats.

"Did you spread the clothes?" said Buttercup.

"I did," said Girl-go-with-the-Goats.

"I hope you've ground the corn at the quern today," said Berry-bright, "for our mother, Dame Dale, will be coming home hungry from the market."

"I have ground the corn at the quern," said Girl-go-with-the-Goats.

"Will you put down a fire and knead and bake a cake for me?" said the Old Woman in the Cloak of Crow-feathers.

"I will," said Girl-go-with-the-Goats.

She went outside and came back with a bundle of sticks. She took down a measure of flour that she had ground at the quern and kneaded a cake. She lit a fire and put the griddle on it. She baked the cake, cut it into four quarters and gave it to the Old Woman.

"Help me over the steppingstones, Brown Girl," said the Old Woman to her then.

"I will," said Girl-go-with-the-Goats. She went outdoors with the Old Woman in the Crow-feather Cloak.

"How that girl shows her ungentility!" said Buttercup. "It is easy knowing the stock she came from by the way she makes up with every beggar and stroller."

"A beggar she herself would be," said Buttercup, "if our mother and ourselves did not give her bread and bed."

6

"She saw her own kind no doubt in Crow-feather Cloak," said Berry-bright. "But call her now, sister, and bring her back, so that she'll have time to cook supper for our mother who must be on her way home by this."

"Really, sister," said Buttercup, "you might go to the door yourself."

"You will have that plate of brass worn out looking at yourself," said Berry-bright.

So Berry-bright and Buttercup spoke to each other: and neither went to the door to call Girl-go-with-the-Goats, who by this time was as far as the steppingstones with the Old Woman in the Crow-feather Cloak.

FRUIT FOR THE KING'S SON

2 ✿ Now WHEN GIRL-GO-WITH-THE-GOATS CAME back from the steppingstones with a shining star on her forehead (and how that star came to be there will be told to you afterward), when she came back to the house of her stepmother, lo and behold! a surprising thing was coming to happen.

For the King's son, no less! had come as far as the garden fornenst that house, and sitting upon his white jennet, he was looking across the ditch into the garden.

And there were Buttercup and Berry-bright standing on the doorstep and making curtsies to

8

him. Girl-go-with-the-Goats stood one side of the garden ditch, letting a bush hide her from the King's son and from her two stepsisters.

"Give me berries out of your garden, fair maids," said the King's son to Berry-bright and to Buttercup. One came toward him and one went back into the house. To the one who came to him he handed a cup of silver.

"Take it into your hand, damsel," he said, "and fill it with berries."

It was Buttercup who had come toward him. She took the silver cup from the King's son and went into the garden. Berry-bright had gone into the house for a vessel, and she came back with an earthenware cup in her hands. When she saw her sister holding the silver cup in her hands she bit her lips in rage.

Buttercup went into the garden. She went to the raspberry bush to pick the berries. But as soon as she came near it, a flock of birds flew at her: sparrows and starlings they were, and they pecked at her eyes and her arms and drove her back to the door of the house.

"Unlucky wench," cried the King's son. "Let

9

the other maid come now and gather me berries in her earthenware cup."

Berry-bright ran toward the red currant bush to pick from it the full of her earthenware cup of berries. But the swallows of the air darted down upon her. With their fierce eyes and wicked mouths they drove Berry-bright out of the garden.

"Unlucky wenches, both," cried the King's son. "Will I not be able to get from your garden a cup full of berries?"

Then Girl-go-with-the-Goats slipped from behind the bush and darted into the garden. She took up an old shoe that lay on the ground. She went toward the black currant bush, and no bird darted in anger at her. Instead two starlings flew down and lighting, one on each shoulder, sang to her. Then Girl-go-with-the-Goats gathered the black currants into the old shoe and took them to the King's son.

"Oh, to be served with black currants out of an old shoe and by a girl as ragged as this wench," cried the King's son. "Out of my sight," he cried when he ate the berries. He took up the old shoe and he struck Girl-go-with-the-Goats on the arm with it.

Still she did not move, but stood looking up at him, her mouth trembling but her eyes steady, and the two starlings resting, one on each shoulder.

"Gawk of a girl, out of my way," cried the King's son. Saying this, he rode his jennet forward and pushed Girl-go-with-the-Goats against the garden ditch.

Then he rode down the road, and the birds that had pecked at Berry-bright and Buttercup flew up into the air.

And there stood Buttercup on the step of the house with the silver cup in her hands, and there stood Berry-bright inside the garden gate with the earthenware cup in her hands, and each one saying to herself, "Who was it that put bad luck on me today?"

And there was Girl-go-with-the-Goats crouching against the garden ditch with the two starlings upon her shoulders, thinking that the very trees around her were singing and that their songs were like the light and like the darkness.

And there was her stepmother, Dame Dale, coming up the path from the steppingstones.

But now we have to tell you how it was that

Girl-go-with-the-Goats came to get that shining star upon her forehead:

A shining star
Like a lonely blossom.

It was the Old Woman in the Crow-feather Cloak who had placed it there for her. They had come together to the steppingstones, the Old Woman holding under her arm the cake that Girl-go-with-the-Goats had kneaded and made and given her. "There is not much I can do for you, Maid-alone," said the Old Woman (for the girl had not called herself Girl-go-with-the-Goats but Maid-alone). "There is not much I can do for you," she said, "except let the world see what I see in you." And saying that, she took water from the stream and splashed it on the girl's forehead. And then came out the shining star. She told the girl to bend down and look at herself in the water of the stream. Girl-go-with-the-Goats bent down and saw the shining star on her forehead. Oh, long and in wonder did she look on it. And when she lifted her face from the flowing stream the Old Woman in the Crow-feather Cloak was not to be seen.

GIRL-GO-WITH-THE-GOATS LOSES HOUSE ROOM

3 ❀ GIRL-GO-WITH-THE-GOATS REMEMBERED ON THE moment what she had to do to make the house well ordered for her stepmother's return. She ran to the door and pushed past her stepsisters and, taking the besom out of the corner, she started to sweep the floor up toward the hearth.

And then she heard Buttercup and Berrybright talking to their mother as they came up the loaning. "Oh, Mother," said Buttercup, "I am as glad to see you as if you had brought a roc's egg to me."

"Oh, what will I say to Dame Dale so that she

will know I am as glad as Buttercup is to see her back?" said Girl-go-with-the-Goats. "A roc's egg! I could never think of anything as magnificent as that!"

"Oh, Mother," said Berry-bright, "I am as glad to see you as if you had brought a phœnix feather to me."

"A phoenix feather!" said Girl-go-with-the-Goats. "I could never think of anything as magnificent as that."

And then Dame Dale was at the doorway. Girl-go-with-the-Goats went on sweeping toward the hearth and her back was toward her. And when she entered the house Dame Dale said, "I have to get the welcome from the hearth yet. And what do you say to me, fosterling?"

Girl-go-with-the-Goats turned round to Dame Dale, the besom in her hands and her face all red with blushes. "I am more pleased to see you," said she, "than if you had brought salt to the house when it was lacking it."

"The idea!" said Buttercup.

"The idea!" said Berry-bright.

But Girl-go-with-the-Goats knew what it was

15

for the house to be without salt for the bread, and salt for the porridge, and salt for the egg. And if the house had been without it there would have been nothing more welcome than salt coming in. But Dame Dale was angry when instead of hearing of a roc's egg and a phœnix feather she heard of salt.

"You are more pleased to see me than if I had brought salt to a house lacking it," she said. "That's to say nothing at all in welcome of me. And it is you who should have given me the welcome from the hearth."

Girl-go-with-the-Goats turned round and swept up the floor and tidied the ashes round the hearth. "She can only think of what goes on her tongue," said Buttercup. "How could fine words or fine thoughts come into her head?"

"It would have been better," said Berry-bright, "if one of your own daughters had stayed within the house to give you a welcome from the hearth."

"How is it," said Dame Dale to Girl-go-with-the-Goats, "how is it that although I have given you good food and good shelter, you never have a good word to say to me?"

16

Girl-go-with-the-Goats did not answer because she could not think of a word to say.

"It was bad enough," said Buttercup, "for her to treat the King's son the way she did."

"Lord!" said Dame Dale, "was the King's son near this?"

"He was at the garden fornenst the door," said Berry-bright. "He wanted berries off our bushes. And we would have brought him the berries in his own silver cup or in one of our best earthenware ones, only nothing would do her except bring him the berries in an old shoe she found in the garden."

"So the King's son rode away from the place in high dudgeon, taking hardly any notice of us," said Buttercup.

"How could such a thing have been let happen?" said Dame Dale.

"Indeed we would not have let it happen if we had known she was there," said Buttercup, "but she hid behind the hedges—we know her way—and we did not see her at all until she was standing before the King's son with the berries in the old shoe."

"The idea of such a thing!" said Dame Dale. "The very idea of it makes me shake with shame."

"Well, she turned the Prince away—and oh, how princely and fine he was looking!—and that ought to be a satisfaction to her," said Berry-bright. "And I know he would have noticed me," she added.

"He certainly would have noticed my hands when I held them up with the cup in them," said Buttercup.

Girl-go-with-the-Goats had now tidied up the ashes around the fire and there was nothing else for her to do but put the besom in the corner and turn round to them. Her face was still red, but on her forehead, like an apple blossom in color, there was a star.

And when she saw the star on the forehead of Girl-go-with-the-Goats Dame Dale had to look from one to the other of her daughters. Neither had a star on her forehead. And Dame Dale saw that the face of Berry-bright was too high-colored and that the face of Buttercup was too pinched. And when she looked back to the star on the forehead of Girl-go-with-the-Goats she got very angry.

"So," said she, "it is that mark on your forehead that makes you too proud to talk to people and too proud to give them a fitting welcome! I suppose you put herbs or blossoms on your forehead to bring that out. But there's no one here who wants to see it. Put your hand in the ashes now and smear that mark across. And keep the smear of ashes on it until the mark has gone away."

Girl-go-with-the-Goats bent down to the ashes and took some on her hand and smeared it across the star on her forehead. But Dame Dale was not pleased either when she turned to her with the star smeared over. Girl-go-with-the-Goats looked like one she should be sorry for. But Dame Dale could not be sorry for her on account of her not giving her a fitting welcome when she came in, and also on account of her having approached the King's son and having on her forehead a star that made her so different from Buttercup and Berry-bright. So instead of being sorry for her when she turned round with the smear of ashes across her forehead, Dame Dale took a more settled dislike to her.

"I wish you out of my sight," she said, "and as you are called go-with-the-Goats, go now and live with the goats. There's the goat shed for you to rest in and sleep in. Come to this hearth no more unless

you are sent for. Your supper and your dinner will
be left for you on the doorstep and as for breakfast,
you can get that for yourself by taking some of the
milk from the goats in the morning. But although

you'll be outside of it, there will be the work of the house that you will still have to do. Go now," said she, "and may all bad temper go with you."

Girl-go-with-the-Goats went outside but she thought she could not bear to go away from the house. So she stood there with her hand against the porch and with her heart heavy within her and her eyes flowing over with tears.

THE *GIRL* IN THE *GOAT SHED*

4   THEY SHUT THE DOOR BEHIND HER AND THEY pulled the latch down on it: she knew that it was either Buttercup or Berry-bright that did this. The latching of the door was like as if someone had pushed her: she went away from the house.

She went from the house and away into the little dell where she used to sit when she wanted to talk to herself. A tree grew in that dell, a rowan tree that had lots of bright red berries on it. She used to sit under that tree when her seven goats hadn't to be minded. She would talk to herself about the clouds and the moon, how the clouds

were great goats that a great goatherd was driving:
first the white fleecy goats and then the dark goats
that went slower and slower, and how the moon
was a girl like herself, having to go far out into the
sky for a pitcher of water. When she was in this dell
she was, not Girl-go-with-the-Goats, but Maid-
alone. And the things that she owned and that she
alone knew of were in that dell: a red bees' nest
that hummed and hummed to her all the hours she
was there; tall bluebells; a little spring of water
that she had set round with the white stones that
she had found on the hill; a flat stone that had the
moving shadow of the leaves, each leaf as clear as
it was on the tree. And she had a box hidden under
the grass; she kept in it all the things that were her
very own: a half of a buckle that looked beautiful
set in a bracelet of grass, four beads of different
colors and a ball of red thread.

She came to that dell and she laid down in the
grass and she cried and cried, for she thought there
was no one in the world as lonely as she. But the
nest of red bees hummed to her and hummed to
her, and she sat up, thinking that her loneliness was
like something she herself had found, her own too,

23

like the half buckle and the beads and the ball of red thread, and the nest of red bees and the blue-bells and the little spring with the white stones round it. She sat up then and she looked at the sky with the clouds going over it and at the bunches of bright red berries on the rowan tree.

Then down from the rowan tree flew the two starlings that had lighted on her shoulders when she gathered the berries for the King's son in the garden. They perched on her shoulders again and they sang to her.

And the song they sang to her was "Down the long meadows we go."

Down the long meadows we go, we go,
Down the long meadows we go.

  I'll pluck you three willow rods down by the
      stream,
  I'll pluck you three willow rods down by the
      stream,
  I'll pluck you three willow rods down by the
      stream,
    And give you the sun that's upon them.

24

A cuckoo all blue will sing on a branch,
A cuckoo all blue will sing on a branch,
A cuckoo all blue will sing on a branch,
  And the swan that's King Connor's will seek
    you.

The son of the King of the Hill will be there,
The son of the King of the Hill will be there,
The son of the King of the Hill will be there,
  Making game of his grandmother's dancing.

Down the long meadows we'll go, we'll go,
Down the long meadows we'll go.

And when Girl-go-with-the-Goats—but Maid-alone she was there—when Maid-alone had heard the song the starlings sang to her she did not feel herself half so lonesome.

And now Girl-go-with-the-Goats rose up, her mind bent on the work of the house that she did not now belong to. When she came before it the door was still closed. Smoke was coming out of the chimney and she knew that supper was being made ready. She brought peat from the stack and left them beside the door so that they could be brought

25

in to the fire. She went and brought up the clothes she had washed and that had been left drying on the stones beside the stream. When she did this she found her supper laid on a board at the gable end of the house, and while she ate it the two starlings perched on her shoulders. Then she took the two pitchers down to the well and brought back the water for the morning.

The next thing was to bring the goats from the high places and the rocky places. She stood on a high place and called to them. One goat lifted her head and came to her. Then three others came, stopping now and again to crop the tops of the little bushes. Beyond the bushes, somewhere, was an old goat that never answered to her call. She had to slip off and find that other one and pull her or drive her to this place before the others found out that she was gone. Then there were two others to get. One she saw on a high rock very far up, but this was a good goat and would come when she called, "Nannie, Nannie, Nannie." The other was a goat without horns and one never knew where she was, but one found her joining the others as they were making for home. Girl-go-with-the-Goats struck the old cantankerous goat with a switch, dodged her horns as she reared up and got her started to the place where most of the other goats had gathered together.

It was hard to get them home. On the way there were scores of little paths, and one goat would try one path and another goat would try another path, and Girl-go-with-the-Goats would have to follow first one and then the other and no sooner would she have them together than they would scatter again. Oh, it was the worst trouble in the whole world, this fending for seven goats!

She got them in the green before the goat shed, and she took off the doorstep the pitcher that she was to milk into. For some reason or another the goats gave little milk that evening and she knew that Dame Dale would say that she had milked them badly or that she spilled their milk.

Then she got the goats into the shed and she took the pitcher and she left it in the stream. It was getting dark now, and as she crossed a wall of stones on her way back a little newt came out from a crack and looked at her. She was frightened of the little creature that is like nothing else in the world,

that moves so strangely and that has its house in the
stones. She might see the door of Dame Dale's
house open, she thought, and Dame Dale standing
there to call her in, now that she had done her
work and that dark night was coming on. But the
door was closed. She waited and waited, but no one
opened it to her. And as she stood there all the
loneliness came back to her and she thought that if
her mother knew that she was standing there with
a door closed to her she would come back from the
dead.

Then Girl-go-with-the-Goats went where the
goats were. A big wooden cradle was in the shed,
the cradle that Buttercup and Berry-bright had
been rocked in, and that had been taken out of the
house. She found the cradle and she lay down in it.
She covered herself all over with dried fern, and she
looked out through the door that would not close.
She thought and thought of the hundreds and hundreds of strange things that were outside. She slept,
but she wakened up sometimes, and she saw the
black goats and the brown goats and the white
goats standing up or lying down, and she wished
that she could be as contented as the goats.

FIRE FOR THE KING'S SON

5   In the morning early she rose up, opened wide the door and let the goats go through. She milked a little from the brown goat and drank the milk for her breakfast. Then she let the seven goats go by themselves off to the high places and the rocky places.

She went down to the stream and she washed her face and her hands. Then she stood on the bank and the two starlings flew down, lighting one on each shoulder, and they began to sing to her. The song they sang was of the little brown jug that she washed every day and left in the center place on the dresser:

Little brown jug,
Don't I love thee?
Bright and brown
Like a kept penny!

I'll fill thee with honey,
I'll fill thee with spice,
I'll border thee with flowers
Of every device.

I'll not let befall thee
A chip or a crack;
I'll leave pewter below thee,
And delph at thy back.

I'll fill thee with spice,
And I'll fill thee with honey,
And I'd not part with thee
For a kettle full of money.

Little brown jug,
Don't I love thee?
Bright and brown
Like a kept penny.

And when the starlings had sung to her, Girl-go-with-the-Goats was not as heavy at heart as she had been before.

Her next stint of work was to take a clappers in her hands and go to the field and frighten the crows from her stepmother's crop. She did this until midday, and then hearing a call for her she went to the house. Dame Dale was at the door. She told Girl-go-with-the-Goats to eat her dinner off the board at the gable end of the house and then go and bring back the seven goats from the high places and the rocky places.

She ate her dinner of bread and milk and an egg. Then she brought the goats home. Her stepmother told her she need not milk them as she had to go to a certain place before the dark of the night came down.

And where had she to go to? To the Forge in the Forest. And what had she to go for? For a pot of fire, no less.

For all that morning Buttercup and Berry-bright, after washing their hands with new milk, sat dizening themselves as before. And Dame Dale, being wearied from her journey, stayed in bed. The consequence of it all was that the fire on the hearth had gone out, and there was no way now of kindling a fire.

And the only place to get fire was at the Forge in the Forest. It wasn't in a forest at all, for the trees had long since been cut down, and where the Forge stood was more of a moorland than a forest. But still it was called the Forge in the Forest, and from all the houses around people went to it for fire when their own hearths were quenched.

And now Girl-go-with-the-Goats was bidden take a pot in her hands and go to the Forge in the Forest for fire for her stepmother's hearth.

She started off, and no sooner had she turned the loaning when the starlings again flew down on her shoulders. And as she went along the path through the wood the two starlings sang to her; whatever she thought of, that they sang to her. She came out on the moorland and when she went a furlong she saw the black Forge. Two Dwarfs with earrings in their ears were within. They took two pieces of glowing wood out of their fire and put them in her pot.

Back she went, hurrying now across the moorland because dark clouds were gathering. As she

went along the path through the wood the starlings on her shoulders twittered their nesting song. The wood was dark around her and she hurried on.

And on the outskirts of the wood she saw a youth gathering kindlings and fagots for a fire. She came face to face with him and she knew him. He was the King's son.

She put down the pot and at once she began gathering kindlings and fagots with him. She brought them where he was bringing his. She laid hers down and built up a fire for him.

"This is the night when, according to my father's councilors, I have to sleep on the moorland," said the King's son. He searched in his wallet. "I had flint and steel," he said, "but I have lost the flint and steel that was to make my fire."

"I have embers," said Girl-go-with-the-Goats. She took the burning embers out of the pot and put them under the wood. A fire began to crackle.

"Leave me now," said the King's son.

"Would you not give me an ember out of the fire I have kindled?" said Girl-go-with-the-Goats.

"I will give you an ember, but not two embers," said the King's son.

She took an ember from the fire. It was not a

weighty ember like one of the two the Dwarfs had given her. It was a light and waning ember. She took it and put it in the pot, thinking she would find fagots on the wayside to kindle beside it.

She went on and on but she found no fagots. And when she looked into her pot again the ember had died out. What was she to do? She walked back, and she saw the fire she had lighted blazing up. She saw the King's son standing beside the fire. She went nearer, but she could hear his voice as he said to her, "I will give you an ember, but not two embers." She was afraid to go near him and have him speak to her again.

She went past the fire and she came to the wood. It was darker and darker. But she put her feet on the path and she went on toward the moorland where the Dwarfs were at work in their forge.

At last she came out of the wood and she went across the moorland, but the forge seemed far and far away. On and on she went, with nothing to sing to her now, and no living thing nearer to her than the bats that flew here and there. And then when she knew she was lost she heard the clank of metal struck. The forge was that way. Now filled with the hope that the Dwarfs would give her embers again and set her upon her way she went on more quickly.

The forge was far away, but at last she was near it. It seemed different from the forge where the Dwarfs worked, higher and wider. She went to the door of the forge. Then, instead of seeing two Dwarfs with earrings in their ears she saw but one person hammering out the links of a chain on the anvil and that person was a red-faced, grizzly bearded Giant.

The Giant saw her. When he looked at her out of his red eyes she dropped the pot and turned and ran. She ran and ran and ran and then she took breath and told herself that no one was chasing her. And then she heard feet scrunching up the ground behind her. She ran on until she fell down. She crept along on her hands and knees and hid behind a bush, thinking he might go scrunching by her. But she heard him snorting and sniffing to smell her out as he came near. She rose up to run again and then she felt his big hands all over her. He wrenched her arms as he picked her up; he slung her across his back and then he went on with her through the black wood.

36

CROW-FEATHER
CLOAK AGAIN

6 ❧ HE CAME OUT OF THE WOODS HOLDING HER BY the legs and carrying her slung across his shoulder. Then with great stride he went up the side of a mountain. He crossed the top and went down the other side so fast that the life was nearly shaken out of her body. But now the Giant lifted Girl-go-with-the-Goats up on his shoulder and his gait was easier for her then.

He went through a gate and into a yard where she heard the yelping and howling of beasts and the rattling of chains. He pushed open the door of a house. He let her down on the ground and closed

37

the door as a boy might let down and shut in the kitten of a wildcat he had taken.

The Giant shut her into the terrible house that was all in darkness. "Don't try to get away, for I'll hear every sound you make," he said to her. Then she heard him cast off his heavy hunting boots and throw down on the ground a chain he carried. She heard him get into his bed. For a while he talked to himself and then she heard him snore in his sleep.

She sat in a corner all the night listening to beasts' feet running, running in the dark before the house. The light came and she saw the house big and empty. She saw the Giant's bed and she saw the Giant lying in it, with his grizzly beard nearly covering his red face. She saw the doors of the house, one at the back and one at the front with bolts on each of them. It was surely a terrible house.

The Giant wakened up. He put his feet under him in the bed and he looked at her. "Ho," said he, "this is the thirtieth maid I have caught. I'll take her to the fastness where I have the other nine-and-twenty."

He opened wide the front door and stood looking into his yard. She stole down and looked out too. A wolf, a wildcat, a fox, a badger—all were running here and there with chains upon them and yelping and howling. The Giant took up the chain he had brought and shook it before the beasts, and they howled and yelped the more angrily.

And then Girl-go-with-the-Goats heard a little twittering in the window opening above her. She looked up and there she saw her two starlings. "Oh, my birds," said she to them softly, "show me, show me some way of escaping from the Giant."

Then the two starlings flew down on the low bench that was by the wall and they shrugged their wings and twisted their heads and went through all the ways of washing themselves. And then they flew up to the window opening, and there again they shrugged their wings and twisted their heads and went through all the ways of washing themselves. Girl-go-with-the-Goats thought she knew what the starlings would have her do: they would have her try to wash herself.

She spoke to the Giant who was still rattling the chain at the beasts. "Mighty man," said she, "would you let me wash myself?"

"Wash yourself and then come with me," said

the Giant. "But I won't let you go out to get the water." He stepped outside the door and came back with a basin of rain water. "Wash now," he said, "and come with me to the fastness where my nine-and-twenty other maids are kept."

She took the basin from him and left it down on the low bench. She stood there not knowing what next to do. And the Giant went to the door as before and made the beasts that were outside yelp and howl with the sight of the chain he held.

And now the two starlings flew down and lighted on the rim of the basin. They began to splash themselves with water. They flew into the basin and splashed louder and louder. Then she knew how the starlings were trying to help her. They would keep splashing and splashing while she stole away from the Giant.

The back door was shut by a bolt of wood that was within her reach. She put up her hands and laid them on the bolt. Louder and louder the starlings splashed in the basin. She pushed the bolt back slowly. She drew the door toward her. With more and more noise the birds splashed in the water.

She opened the door a little way. She stepped

out and closed the door behind her. She stopped to listen. She heard the starlings in the basin of water splashing and splashing and splashing.

And then Girl-go-with-the-Goats ran on, ran on. Far, far she went before she stopped to drink at a stream or pick a berry. Along a pathway in a wood she went, fearful because she did not know where she was going.

It was then she heard two magpies discoursing to one another in human language: "When was your tongue split with a silver sixpence so that you were made able to speak in men's language?" said one to the other.

"It was before the night of the great wind," said the second magpie. "That same great wind blew myself and my cage away and ever since I'm in these woods. And when was your tongue split?"

"Mine was split before the battle in the sky was seen," said the first magpie. "The people in the house ran out to see the same battle and I hopped off my perch and came away."

"And when you want to speak human words to whom do you go?" said the second magpie.

"Oh, to no one else but the Woman of a Thousand Years," said the first magpie. "Her house is down by this pathway."

"I go to talk to the Little Green Man of the Mountain," said the second magpie. The two went hopping off together.

Girl-go-with-the-Goats went along the path that the first magpie had spoken of. She did not go far before she saw a small black house deep-sunken in the earth, with elder bushes growing around it. The door of the house was open, and she stole up so that she might first look to see who was within.

An Old Woman was there spinning threads of gray on a spindle. The only garment she had on was a Cloak of Crow-feathers. She went in on the doorway. "Good evening," said she to the Old Woman.

The Old Woman in the Crow-feather Cloak looked at her from under her gray eyebrows. "Good evening, girl that I remember," she said.

"May I come in and rest myself?" said Girl-go with-the-Goats.

"Come in and rest yourself," said the Woman of a Thousand Years.

Girl-go-with-the-Goats came into that little

house, and oh, but her heart was rested to be within a house that was not fearful to her. She sat down on a stool, and the moment she did she began to think of her stepmother's goats. Where were they, and who was minding them today?

"Girl that I remember, would you eat or drink?" said the Woman of a Thousand Years.

"I would take a drink of milk if you could spare it," said Girl-go-with-the-Goats.

"There's no milk in the house, but this may do as well," said the old woman. She brought the girl a bowl of elderberry wine; dark red and sharp-smelling it was. She drank the bowl of wine and the fears that she still had began to go away from her.

And then the two starlings flew into the house and lighting on the window sill behind her began to sing loudly and joyfully. Oh, it was well to be here in this house, with the bowl in her hands and the two starlings singing. She laid her head against the wall, and no sooner did she do this than she fell into slumber.

THROUGH THE THREE WOODS AND TO THE KING'S CASTLE

7 WHEN SHE WOKE UP IT WAS EVENING; THE crickets were singing in the ashes on the hearth, the rush candle was lighted and the Woman of a Thousand Years was sitting on the other side of the fire supping her whey.

She heard a clatter before the door, and then a strange creature came in. The look of him made Maid-alone afeared, but the Woman of a Thousand Years said, "Take no heed of him; he is the Gruagach that I call Trouble-the-House."

He had horse's legs, but for all that he was not as tall as a horse would be if it stood up. He had the ears of a horse too, but he had the face of a poor-spirited man. He sidled to the dresser, and he took down a brass plate and the tin covers, and he began to polish them with a napkin that was hanging on the line. He sidled to the fire then and sat before it, his horse's legs folded under him like a tailor's. He wore a long coat that was made of plaited rushes and he had hairy arms and big hands that he clasped behind his neck when he sat down.

No one spoke to him and he spoke to no one, and in a while he got up and took the pail and went out. When he was gone the Woman of a Thousand Years said, "If you can catch him while he is doing some stint of work, and lay your command on him, he will carry you through the Three Woods. But you will have to come upon him and speak to him while he is doing some task."

Trouble-the-House brought back a pail full of water and then went out of the door. Maid-alone heard the clatter of his hoofs outside, and the Woman of a Thousand Years told her he had gone off to sleep in the middle of a field of furze bushes. "Catch him tomorrow while he's doing some task," she said, "and he will carry you to the place you would go."

Then the Woman of a Thousand Years took off her Cloak of Crow-feathers, and she wrapped herself in a quilt of small birds' feathers and gave another quilt to Maid-alone, and they spread out the rushes and the moss, and they laid down and went to sleep.

Maid-alone dreamed of her stepmother's goats and of the Giant and his beasts, and then she wakened. When she went to sleep again she was happy that she was in a quiet house with only the stir of the crickets to trouble her rest.

The Woman of a Thousand Years rose first, and she went out to wash her face in the dew of the morning. When she came back her eyes were bright and her step was quick. "Maid-alone," said she, "I have thought of what is to befall you. You must make no delay but go to the King's Castle. Find Trouble-the-House and lay the command on him that he is to take you there through the Three Woods."

Maid-alone, without waiting to eat her crust, went out to look for Trouble-the-House. He was in the field of furze bushes where he had slept the night. His coat of plaited rushes was off, and he was brushing from his hide the thorns and prickles of the furze. Maid-alone went straight to him, but he rose up and went clattering away.

She went back to the house of the Woman of a Thousand Years and ate her crust and drank her bowl of elderberry wine. Again she went to find Trouble-the-House, and she came upon him as he was grinding oats at the quern stone. When he saw her on her way he rose and betook himself to the field of the furze bushes. For the rest of the day he did no work, and every time Maid-alone came on him he was lying on his back, idling his time.

This is what the Woman of a Thousand Years told her to do: she was to sit by the fire with the Crow-feather Cloak about her so that Trouble-the-House would think that only the woman was there. And when he was fixing the fire she was to catch hold of his plaited rush coat and lay her command on him to carry her through the Three Woods and to the King's Castle.

So Maid-alone put on the Cloak of Crow-feathers and the Woman of a Thousand Years put on her brown habit and sat with her back to the brown wall; in the little light made by the rush candle she wasn't to be seen at all.

Then Trouble-the-House came clattering to

the door. He went to the dresser and took down the
brass plate and the tin covers and he polished them
with the napkin that was hanging on the line. He
threw side looks at the fire, and when he saw that it
was burning low he came to it, and squatting down
before it put kindlings in. Maid-alone laid her
hands on his coat of plaited rushes and she said:
"You must carry me through the Three Woods and
to the King's Castle this very night."

"I'll carry you, I'll carry you since so you'll
have it," said the Gruagach, and he rose up and
went out.

"Go to him now," said the Woman of a Thousand Years. "You'll find him where he's taking a
drink of water at the well. Through the Three
Woods you will go: the Wood of Bronze, the Wood
of Silver and the Wood of Gold. Pluck a twig in
each wood no matter what the Gruagach says to
you, and make him carry whatever the twig turns
into. When you come to the King's Castle go into it
by the least grand way, wearing the Crow-feather
Cloak that I now bestow on you."

The rush candle went out, and Maid-alone saw
no more of the Woman of a Thousand Years. She
went out of the door, and to the well, and she saw

the Gruagach there taking a drink of water. She bade him take her to the King's Castle, through the three Woods, and to make good speed. He stooped down and she got upon his back.

They went on and on until they came to the Wood of Bronze. The moon was clear in the sky and it showed the glitter of the leaves and the twigs and the branches. One wakeful blackbird was flying and crying through that wood as Maid-alone and the Gruagach went on.

Then remembering what the Woman of a Thousand Years had told her to do, Maid-alone put up her hand and broke off a glittering twig with its glittering leaves. The Gruagach pinched her hands saying: "Beaten I'll be coming back through this wood for the thing you have done, girl. Break off no more twigs or I'll leave you on the ground."

But the twig she had broken off turned into a glittering dress, with a glittering veil and a pair of glittering shoes, and Maid-alone forgot the pinches that the Gruagach gave her, such delight was hers.

They came to a second wood. Still the moon was clear in the sky and the leaves and twigs shone white and bright. A wakeful cuckoo was crying in

the wood, and as they went on Maid-alone broke
off a silver twig with silver leaves.

It turned into a silver dress with a silver veil
and a pair of silver shoes. Maid-alone left it on the
Gruagach's shoulders with the dress of glittering
bronze. But Trouble-the-House, when he knew
what she had done, shook her until she was dizzy.
"Beaten I'll be when I come back through this
wood for the thing you have done," said he. "Break
off no more twigs, break off no more twigs, or I'll
leave you down to go your way by yourself." Maid-
alone forgot the shaking he gave her, such delight
was hers at the sight of the silver dress beside the
bronze one.

They came into the third wood. The moon
was still clear in the sky, and it showed leaves soft
as candle flames and twigs that were rods of bright-
ness. A nightingale sang in that wood, and its song
was like the moonlight on the leaves.

Maid-alone was afeared that the Gruagach
would leave her alone in that wood if she broke off
a twig with leaves and for a long time she would
not put up her hand to break one off. But she might
not leave that wood without taking a golden twig
with its golden leaves. Then as they were coming

52

out of the thick of the wood she reached up and broke off a shining twig with its shining leaves.

The Gruagach slapped her with his great hands. "Beaten I'll be in every wood I go through for what you have done, girl."

But Maid-alone did not heed the beating he gave her. For the twig and the leaves turned into a shining dress, with a shining veil and a pair of shining shoes. This dress, too, she put across the Gruagach's shoulders, and the two went on.

After they came out of the Three Woods they went across seven ridges, but Maid-alone did not heed the distance they traveled, for her mind was on the three fine dresses that were before her, the gleaming and glittering and shining dresses. They came to a white river and they heard cocks crowing, more cocks than ever Maid-alone heard crow together before. And looking hard in the direction that the cocks were crowing she saw the roofs of the King's Castle. The Gruagach put her down on the ground and he left her dresses beside her. Then he loosened his coat of plaited rushes, took it off and putting it across his shoulder started running back along the way they had come. Maid-alone was left standing beside a great tree.

WATER FOR THE KING'S SON

8 ✿ THE TREE SHE WAS BESIDE HAD A HOLLOW IN
it, a hollow wide and clean and dry. She put
pegs in the hollow and she hung up her dresses
there, the bronze dress, the silver dress and the
golden dress.

Then Maid-alone went in the direction in
which she heard the peacocks cry. She came to the
King's Castle with its stables and its kennels, with
its mews for hawks and its meres for herons, with
its ponds for swans and its parades for peacocks.
She came to the King's Castle, and she found the
least grand way to enter it and she went that way

54

and stood before the grille that was in the lowest door. When she knocked, the third of the understewardesses opened the grille and looked out at her.

"What do you want, girl in the Crow-feather Cloak?" said the third of the understewardesses.

"To work in the King's Castle," said Maid-alone.

Then the third of the understewardesses said to her, "Can you mind geese, girl?"

"Geese would be easy for me to mind," said Maid-alone.

"Then come to me after the plowmen go into the fields and I'll take you to the goose shelter," said the third of the understewardesses.

She closed the grille, but Maid-alone stayed there until she saw the plowmen go into the fields. She knocked again, and the third of the understewardesses opened the lowest door in the Castle and brought her into the scullery and gave her crusts and scraps for her breakfast.

Then she brought Maid-alone to the wide shelter where two score geese were lifting up their necks and shaking out their wings and clangoring.

She gave her the rod of the gooseherd and told her to take the goose flock down to the marsh.

When the geese were all feeding in the marsh with one gander to watch for them, Maid-alone left them for a while and came out on the highway. Along the highway a coach with four horses was coming. And at a distance from the coach a horseman was riding with a hound running beside him.

When the coach came near where she was standing it stopped, and out of it stepped two damsels grandly dressed. They were Maid-alone's foster sisters, Berry-bright and Buttercup. There was a third person in the coach and she was Dame Dale, Maid-alone's foster mother.

"It is the King's son who is riding behind us on his high-mettled horse," said Dame Dale to the damsels. "Stand beside the coach now, my fair daughters, and give him the chance of looking at you."

Buttercup and Berry-bright stood alongside the coach in their grand dresses and the King's son came riding up to them.

"Is there aught we can do to serve you, noble lord?" said Berry-bright. The King's son drew the

56

rein of his high-mettled horse and his bell-mouthed hound stayed by him. "Is there aught we can do to serve you, noble lord?" said Buttercup.

"If you would serve me, damsels," said the King's son, "bring me a drink of water from the cold well yonder."

"We have no vessel to bring the water to you, good lord," said Berry-bright.

"Your own beautiful white hands will do to carry the water in," said Dame Dale from the coach.

Berry-bright started off for the well, and Maid-alone in her Crow-feather Cloak, unseen and un-known by them all, stood near and looked on.

Berry-bright came back with her fingers knit together and her palms hollowed out to hold the water. The King's son slipped down from his horse to drink and the hands that were made white with washings in new milk were held up to him. The face of Berry-bright was red with pride and the face of Buttercup was white with envy.

But when he stooped down to drink, the water had flowed away. He lifted his head and he turned away from her.

Then Buttercup started for the well. She came back with her fingers knit and her palms hollowed to hold the water. She held up the hands that were white with washings in new milk, and the red of pride was on her face.

But from her hands, too, the water flowed away, and after he had bent down to empty palms the King's son lifted his head and turned away from her.

Maid-alone stole to the well. She came back with her fingers knit and her palms hollowed to hold the water. The water stayed within her firm hands, and the King's son stooped down and drank all that was held there. Dame Dale and Berry-bright and Buttercup looked on the girl in the Crow-feather Cloak and knew her for Maid-alone who had minded their goats.

And the King's son looked on her and on her queer Cloak of Crow-feathers. He looked on her once, and he looked on her again. "He is wondering what hole she came out of," said Dame Dale to her daughters.

"Bring water for my hound to dip his tongue in," said the King's son.

Maid-alone went to the well again and came back with water in the hollow of her palms. She stooped down and the King's son's hound put his tongue into the water and then lapped it up. The King's son mounted his high-mettled horse and he rode off with his bell-mouthed hound running beside him.

Berry-bright and Buttercup said not a word to Maid-alone. They stepped into the coach and seated themselves beside Dame Dale and the coach drove off toward the King's Castle.

And as for Maid-alone, she went back to where her goose flock was feeding in the marsh and she watched over them. Then when the sun was near sinking she gathered them together and drove them across the fields to the goose shelter near the Castle. When she was eating her supper of scraps in the scullery she heard the news of the Castle. The King's son was soon to choose a wife, and all the maidens of the land were being gathered for him to look at; they would be lodged in the fifty-five new chambers of the Castle. Two had come that day, arriving in the fourth royal coach, and their mother, Dame Dale, was to be the new house dame.

WHAT THE
GEESE TALKED OF

9 ✿ ON THE MORNING OF THE NEXT DAY MAID-
alone went into the goose shelter, and the two
score geese when they saw her amongst them
stretched up their necks, shook out their wings and
set up their goose gabble. She had the rod of the
gooseherd in her hand and she drove them out, set-
ting the ganders marching at the heads of their
companies.

She took them to the marsh, and she waited
till they had all settled down to feed, leaving a
gander to watch and ward for them. Then she hurried from the marsh and went to the hollow tree

60

where her dresses were hidden; she took off her Crow-feather Cloak and she put on the first of her fine dresses, the glittering dress of bronze, with the gleaming shoes and the glittering veil.

She hung up the Crow-feather Cloak on the peg that the first of her fine dresses had been on. Then she went back to the swamp where the geese were feeding. The watcher and the warder for the flock saw her coming and he set up his cry. The other geese looked up and saw her. They stretched up their necks and they shook out their wings, and they cackled and clamored and crowed around her. And whether she sat down on the stump of a tree or walked about in the sunlight, the geese crowded round or followed her.

No goose fed, and no gander kept watch or ward. Their necks were stretched up all the time she was there in her gleaming dress, with her glittering veil and gleaming shoes. And one goose kept saying that she was like a beautiful poplar tree, and another that she was like a shining water lily. And an old goose kept saying that she was like Helen of Greece that her grandmother had told her about, Helen of Greece who was born out of a swan's egg.

62

So the geese kept on talking with their necks stretched up. They neither fed nor kept watch from the time she came amongst them in her bronze dress. And when it was near sunset, Maid-alone turned to go to the hollow tree to leave back the first of her fine dresses and put on the Crow-feather Cloak. The geese followed her. She ran ahead of the flock and she had the bronze dress off and the Crow-feather Cloak on before they came to where she was standing at the hollow tree. She drove them back to the goose shelter, and they went on with their heads held high, telling of the wondrous maiden they had seen in the marsh. And one kept saying that she was like a beautiful poplar tree, and another kept saying that she was like a shining water lily. But the oldest of the geese kept saying that she was like Helen of Greece that her grand-mother had told her about, Helen of Greece who was born out of a swan's egg.

THE KING'S SON GOES SEEKING

10 ❀ AND THAT IS HOW THE KING'S SON CAME TO hear of the beauty of the maiden who had no name.

His Muime—that is, his ancient foster mother —had a dormer room above the goose fold. She wakened up before the shriek of day and she heard the geese tell of the beauty of the maiden who had on a gleaming dress, with a glittering veil and gleaming shoes. The King's son's ancient foster mother listened to it all. She was a wise woman and she knew that the geese had seen what they were speaking of; for the token was that they had eaten next to nothing in the marsh.

She went to the King's son and she said to him: "Make no hasty choice, son of King Daniel. The maiden you wed should be one that the moon would bow down to. And I want to tell you that the geese in the goose fold are telling of one who has such beauty. You would be lucky if you could find her, and my advice to you is that you mount on your horse and ride to all places where the geese have been."

So his Muime said to the King's son. Now the first company of maidens had come that very day and they were being lodged in the fifty-five new chambers in the King's Castle. They had invited the King's son to play blindman's buff up and down the stairs with them; but he listened to what his ancient foster mother told him, and although he had on the knee breeches that best showed his legs he sent a message asking to be excused from the game, and he mounted his horse and rode off to find the maiden that the geese made such a clamor about.

Maid-alone came to the goose fold that morning wearing her Crow-feather Cloak. She drove the geese to the marsh, but knowing they would not feed if she had on any of her fine dresses she made no change in her garb.

The King's son went riding by on his high-mettled horse. He saw the white geese and the gray geese feeding in great contentment with one of the ganders a little way off keeping watch and ward. A girl was standing there herding the goose flock, and her bare feet were in the marsh water. The King's son rode by.

And the next morning, though she came to her dormer window to listen, the King's son's ancient foster mother heard no talk of a maiden that was as beautiful as a poplar tree, or a shining water lily or as that queen in Greece that one's grandmother remembered. The light-minded geese had forgotten what they had talked about.

But they came to clamor again. The next day Maid-alone left the flock feeding in the marsh with a gander to keep watch and ward, and she went to the hollow tree and took out the second of her fine dresses. All in silver was she clad now, with a shimmering veil and glimmering shoes.

And what befell before befell again. No goose fed that day and no gander kept watch and ward.

66

With their necks stretched out they told each other of her beauty. They said the same things as they said before. But this time they made twice as much clamor.

When it was near sunset Maid-alone turned to go to the hollow tree. The goose flock followed her. She ran ahead, and she had the silver dress off and the Crow-feather Cloak on before they came to where she was standing.

But they kept up the clamor in the goose fold. They wakened up the King's son's ancient foster mother before the stars had waned in the sky. She heard about the beauty of the maiden who was all clad in silver, and who was more lovely than a poplar tree, or a shining water lily or that queen in Greece that one's grandmother remembered.

"What a loss it will be," said his Muime to the King's son, "if you miss marrying the beauty that the geese go hungry from thinking about."

He was sitting in the King's Council Chamber with the King's Councilors around him. And what they were trying to decide was whether it was the first or the second company of maidens—the second company had just come—that had the right to entertain him to the game of throwing the apple.

"A loss it would be indeed," said the King's son, "if such a one were near and I missed fixing my choice on her." He went out of the Council Chamber and he mounted his horse and he rode to the marsh where Maid-alone was minding her goose flock. If she had on then her bronze or her silver dress he would have been sure to notice her.

But there she was standing with her Crow-feather Cloak on and her bare feet in the marsh water. The King's son looked at her and rode on to his father's Castle.

That day the geese fed in great contentment, and the ganders kept watch and ward in their regular order, for there was nothing for a goose flock to stretch up necks to. But the next day Maid-alone put on the third of her fine dresses, her dress of gold, with her shining veil and her golden shoes. She went back to the marsh in that attire.

No goose fed and no gander kept watch. The goose flock told each other the things they had told when she had on her bronze dress and when she had on her silver dress. This time they made three times the clamor they made before. The King's son's ancient foster mother was kept awake all night. When the morning came she went to the King's son, and she told him that he would never have any luck in his life if he did not go off at once and search for the beauty that gave two score geese cause for such clamor.

He was then standing on the steps of his father's Castle, ready to receive the third company of maidens that were coming that very day. But he mounted his horse and rode off again. And he saw a girl with a Crow-feather Cloak upon her and with gray geese and white geese standing around her. And when he saw that sight he rode back to his father's Castle and he told his Muime that that was the last time he would ride out to seek the maiden that was without a name.

HOW *MAID-ALONE* CEASED BEING A *GOOSEHERD*

II ❧ THE NEXT HAPPENING WAS THAT THE PUR-
veyor to the King's Castle took stock of the
goose flock.

He had to have geese of size for the feasts that
were to be given in the Castle. He watched Maid-
alone's flock coming home and he saw that they
were as thin as corn crakes when they first come
into the meadows. He notified the third under-
stewardess of this and the third understewardess
went and told the house dame. Thereupon the
house dame said that she herself would go and
speak to the gooseherd.

70

Maid-alone was standing before the table in the scullery eating her supper of scraps, with the cold of the marsh still in her bones. The day before the goose flock had not fed because she had shown herself in her dress of gold, with her shining veil and her golden shoes. This day she had worn her Crow-feather Cloak. But because two eagles had come into the ash trees beside the marsh and had remained watching them all day, the geese had not fed. When they went home there was two days' hunger upon them and they had a thinness that might be measured.

Dame Dale came down to the scullery to speak to the gooseherd about it, and greatly surprised was she to see that the gooseherd was no other than Maid-alone who had herded her goats. She had on a high-coifed linen cap, and her face grew very red beneath it when she looked on Maid-alone. "So," she said, "you left my seven goats straying to come here to let the King's geese go starving. Wherever you are there are losses. But what you've done here is the worst of all, and if you were in the dominions of any other King but this you would surely be tried for malfeasance; for to let the King's geese starve

71

is a step toward overthrowing the royal realm."

The high cap on her head shook with anger. Maid-alone had never seen her so terrible. She towered up in her authority and Maid-alone thought she would order her to be thrown into a pit of serpents. She wished that Trouble-the-House was near to carry her from the Castle.

And then she saw that Dame Dale's eyes were fixed upon the star on her forehead. It was not smeared over. The look in Dame Dale's eyes frightened her so much that she felt sorry the star had ever been given her.

"I'll not let the geese go hungry again," she said.

"We'll see that you won't," said Dame Dale. "We'll get some one else to take them to the marsh. We can't have the King's geese go low in flesh and high in bone just because you want to disport yourself in the marsh to wherever else you take them to." She turned to the third understewardess, and she said, "I require you to get another herd for the King's geese by tomorrow morning."

"I'll go away," said Maid-alone, not knowing where in the world she could go.

72

"I forbid you to leave the King's Castle," said Dame Dale. "There's work here that has to be done. We have no one to clear out the ashes of the seven kitchens, and if you're good for nothing else you'll do for a cinder-wench. Go, on this instant, down to the lower kitchens and take the task of keeping the hearths clear of ashes."

And that is how it came that Maid-alone, instead of going to the marsh with the goose flock, stayed in the underground kitchens of the King's Castle. There had been no cinder-wench for long, and the ashes were deep on the hearths of the seven kitchens. Maid-alone had to gather the ashes and to draw them to the great ash heap outside. Soon her Crow-feather Cloak was all gray with ashes. And the soot drops from the chimneys fell on her hands and her face. She was black with the soot and gray with the ashes, and the servants in the Castle would not let her come to eat in the scullery. She had to take her dish and her porringer on her knee and sit and eat by one or the other of the great hearths. They would let her have no place to sleep near them and she had to huddle herself by one of the hearths and go to sleep over the ashes.

73

THE GIRL WHO SAT BY THE ASHES

12 ❀ SHE SAW NO MORE OF HER WHITE AND GRAY goose flock, no more of the green meadows they went marching through, no more of the great clouds that were above her when she stood in the marsh. She heard no more the nuthatches calling to each other in the bushes and the ash trees around. Always she was going from one kitchen to another, carrying her tub of ashes, and the outlandish servants who were there never spoke to her. And at night when she sat by one of the fires there wasn't a cat there to keep her company. There were crickets there, to be sure, crickets aplenty, but she didn't

74

like them, for they got in her hair when she slept by the fire at night.

The Ratcatcher was the only one who spoke to her. Once he showed her a salamander that lived in the fire and he told her what to say when one sees a salamander:

> *Little lizard of the fire,*
> *Will you stay and look at me?*
> *No, you will not; you will go*
> *Like a word that's said.*
>
> *Only dust of diamonds flung*
> *On your tail,*
> *Little lizard that breathes flame,*
> *Makes you stay.*

Often and often she looked into that fire, but she never saw the salamander again.

Away down a long passage there was a draw well that was covered over by a great stone. When all the outlandish servants had gone out of the great kitchens, Maid-alone would go down to the end of that passage, clear off the stone and draw a pail of water from the depths. Maid-alone could not see to the water. But she would let a pail down and draw

75

it up filled. Then she would wash herself clear of the soot and the ashes and she would comb her hair with a comb she had made, bristles stuck in a piece of wood. Then for an hour she would be clean and fair, and the star upon her forehead was to be seen. But no one ever saw her at that hour.

Then a great stroke would go through all the Castle. It was the Tower Clock striking one. The outlandish servants would troop in to make ready for the baking of the bread and the meats for the morning meal. Maid-alone would then have to clear the ashes from the seven hearths. Her Crow-feather Cloak would become grayer with the ashes, her hands and her face would be spotted with the soot from the chimneys and the ashy crickets of the hearth would be in her hair.

THE *BALL* IN THE *KING'S* *C*ASTLE

13 ❦ No one knew how many twisted stairways and crooked passageways led from the underground kitchens up into the main hallway of the King's Castle. But when you were in the hallway you saw before you the great sweeping scarlet staircase that went up to the grandest chambers. Every night seven servitors, dressed in velvets, stood on that staircase, ten steps apart, each holding a silver candlestick of seven branches in his hands to light the way to the grand chambers.

And in the grandest of the grand chambers, in the Solar Gallery, no less, a ball was being held that was the grandest ever given in the royal realm; it was being given by the King to the maidens who had come to the Castle and from amongst whom the King's son was to choose a wife. He was not required to make his choice at this ball; there were to be three and at the finish of the third ball he was to make his choice.

There were a thousand candles lighted in the gallery, but if there had not been one lighted the gallery would have been bright because of the hanging lusters and the standing silvers that were there. There were citrons and pomegranates heaped on the table, there were seventeen fiddlers wearing cocked hats in the little gallery and all the maidens who came to the ball were required to wear grass-green slippers so that their feet might look well on the cloth-of-gold carpet.

Dame Dale gave her last commands to the underservants, and then she ordered a page to go to her two daughters, Berry-bright and Buttercup, and request them to come to her in her own chamber. The damsels came with the page behind them carrying the boxes in which were the dresses they were to wear at the ball. Dame Dale dressed them from

79

shoe tie to necklace. The wreaths they brought she would not have them wear; she sent out to the King's garden for roses of the white and red, and she made fresh wreaths for them. She gave each a new, perfumed pocket handkerchief and a fan made out of swan's feathers.

"I do not know," she said, "which of you is the better favored, but the King's son would make a good choice if he should choose either of you."

Berry-bright looked at Buttercup and she thought that it would be a pity indeed if the King's son was misled into choosing her, and Buttercup looked at her sister and thought that somebody ought to mention to the King's son that she had a cast in her eye which she managed to conceal very unfairly.

"Pray, Mother," said Buttercup, "why do you let people from the underground kitchens come out into the main hallway? I met the Ratcatcher with his cage of brown rats and I thought I should expire with disgust."

"The Ratcatcher will have to stay below with the other servants, including our own housemate, Girl-go-with-the-Goats," said Dame Dale.

"Is she in the King's Castle?" asked Berry-bright. "I should have thought, Mother, you would have done something to keep her at a distance. You know she might claim kin with us."

"She is the cinder-wench below stairs, and we have said enough about her," said Dame Dale.

She rubbed the cheeks of each of her daughters with a hare's foot to bring out the color, she put nosegays bound with bright ribbons in their hands and she took them along passages and brought them out in the main hall, just in front of the great, sweeping, scarlet staircase.

Then up the great scarlet staircase Buttercup and Berry-bright went, each holding her nosegay high in her hand. The seven servitors, dressed in velvets, holding the silver candlesticks of seven branches, lighted the way for them. And nine captive nightingales, in darkened cages, were singing in the alcoves along the stairs.

Buttercup and Berry-bright entered the Solar Gallery, and they curtsied to the right to the King's son and to the left to the Peers who were there. All the young Peers of the Realm were at the ball, but it was expected that no one less than a Duke would ask any of the maidens to dance with him.

A score of servants came in and scattered rose

leaves over the floor. Then the seventeen fiddlers tuned up their instruments and played the Laughter Tune, and if there were any there who were not gay before, they were made gay then. The King's son took off his diadem and the Peers of the Realm took off their velvet cloaks, and the maidens in their robes of gauze and spangle, of silk and satin, walked around in procession. The King's son and the Peers of the Realm held their hands high for the procession to pass under; the King's son took the hand of the last maiden, and the dance began.

Whoever had known him before would hardly have known him now, so changed was the King's son. He forgot all the importance that conversation with people in authority had given him. He laughed as he danced and he danced as he laughed. He thought that each of his partners was the only matchless maiden in the world. He would not have to make his choice now, he knew; however, at the close of the ball he would have to ask the maiden who he thought was the fairest to distribute the citrons and pomegranates amongst the company.

The King's son danced with dark-haired maidens, and fair-haired maidens, and brown-haired maidens. At last he came to dance with Berry-bright. He admired the beauty of her white hands, and he thought that she would be the one he would choose to distribute the citrons and pomegranates amongst the company. But then he danced with Buttercup, and he thought that she was the one he would ask to do it. For Buttercup had lovely curls just touching her shoulders, and her conversation was very pleasing.

And after he had danced with Buttercup there was a lull in the music. The Chamberlain approached him and began to tell him of the points of beauty that each maiden showed as she displayed herself in the dance. But just then he noticed that all the young Peers of the Realm were standing with their hands shading their eyes to look at someone who had come into the gallery.

A maiden she was, and she wore a dress of bronze, a gleaming dress, with a glittering veil and gleaming shoes. She was slender and her white arms and her dark hair were lovely to behold. On her forehead was a star, in her cheek was a dimple and on her mouth was a smile of eagerness and joy.

She curtsied to the right to the King's son and

she curtsied to the left to the Peers of the Realm. The Dukes whispered to the lesser Peers. The King's son stood bewildered. The Chamberlain dropped the notes he had made, for here was a maiden who had points of beauty exceeding all that the other maidens had put together.

Then the King's son collected himself and went to her. "Where have you come from, bright damsel?" he said.

"I came from Ditchland which is by Old Shoe Garden," she said.

"And will you dance with me?" said the King's son.

"When you rede aright where I've come from," said she.

The King's son drew back from her, not knowing what to say, and the most admired of the young Dukes came and took her hand and led her into the dance.

When it was over the King's son went to her again. But now there was a lull in the music, and the fiddlers did not tune up for another dance. "Dancing is over," said the King's son, "but I beg of you to come to the table and distribute the citrons and pomegranates amongst the company."

Then the new-come maiden walked up to the table, and those who were little looked over the others' shoulders to see her pass. She took a citron and a pomegranate in each hand and very graciously she offered them to one of the maidens. She took another citron and another pomegranate and she brought them over to another maiden. She took a great many citrons and pomegranates and was bringing them to this one and that one in the company, when suddenly there came a heavy sound into the gallery. It was the Clock in the Tower striking twelve. The new-come maiden let the citrons and the pomegranates fall, and they rolled upon the floor. She ran to the wide doorway. Before any one knew that she was out of the gallery she was speeding down the scarlet stairway, past the seven servitors holding their branched candlesticks, and down into the main hall. They saw her in the hallway. But when the King's son with the Peers of the Realms, the seventeen fiddlers, and the score of servants who had strewn the rose leaves came into the hallway, the maiden with the gleaming dress, the glittering veil and the gleaming shoes was nowhere to be seen.

86

THE MATCHLESS MAIDEN LOSES HER GOLDEN SLIPPER

14 ✿ HERE, THE MAIDENS WERE WALKING IN THE King's garden, gathering roses of the white and red, and telling each other about this and that that was said at the ball, and about such and such that was worn; there, Maid-alone, seated by the ashy hearth, was eating her luncheon of scraps and listening to the Ratcatcher complain against the servants for saying that he was letting the rats eat up all the tallow that they had for candles; and yonder, in her lady's chamber, Dame Dale sat listening to what her daughters, Berry-bright and Buttercup, were saying about the strange maiden who was the last to come into the King's ball.

"She came late and she sped away before the end to start people talking about her," said Buttercup.

"And her slippers!" said Berry-bright. "Was it noticed, I wonder, that her slippers were bronze-colored? That one should come to the ball not wearing grass-green slippers was an affront to the Chamberlain who had arranged everything to bring out the gold on the ground."

"Nobody seemed to notice that she spoiled the whole ball. Everything was going very agreeably before she came in," said Buttercup. "And the King's son would have asked me to distribute the citrons and pomegranates: that is one thing I am sure of."

"You need not be so sure of that, sister," said Berry-bright. "I saw him look from the citrons and pomegranates to my white hands, and I know for a surety what was passing in his mind."

Outside the King's son was looking over the garden wall to see if the maiden who came last to the ball was with the others. And not seeing her there he sighed and rode away.

88

And at that very moment the Chamberlain had finished writing down the points of beauty of the maidens who were present, and all the points of beauty that the maiden in the bronze dress had. She had no name that he knew of, but opposite her count he wrote: The Matchless Maiden.

Then the evening breeze came and shook the strings of the little bells of silver that were hung across the Solar Gallery; the little bells chimed and chimed, wakening the nine nightingales in their darkened cages. The nightingales all began to sing. The score of servants came in and lighted the thousand candles and scattered the rose leaves on the cloth-of-gold carpet. Then the seven servitors took their places upon the great scarlet stairway, standing ten steps apart, each holding a silver candlestick of seven branches in his hand.

All in their gauzes and spangles and laces the maidens began to come up the grand stairway. They all wore in their hair the high combs that the King's mother had given them for presents, and each had a rose behind her ear. When the maidens had taken a turn in the Solar Gallery the King's son and the young Peers of the Realm came up the stairway, the King's son with the diadem on his head, and all the Peers with velvet cloaks, and the Dukes wearing diamond buckles in their shoes. Berry-bright and Buttercup did not go up the stairs with the rest of the maidens; when the others were in the Solar Gallery they came in; gracefully, as their mother had taught them, they curtsied to the right to the King's son and to the left to the Peers of the Realm.

That night there were more musicians than the seventeen fiddlers in the little gallery. They all tuned up their instruments and played the Laughter Tune, and if there were any there who were not gay before they were made gay now. The King's son took off his diadem and the Peers of the Realm took off their velvet cloaks and the maidens in their robes of gauze and spangle, of silk and satin, walked round in procession. The King's son and the Peers of the Realm held their hands high for the procession to pass under; the King's son took the hand of the last maiden, and the dance began.

The King's son and all the Dukes would have been looking over their shoulders to the entrance of the Gallery to watch for some one else, only there was a fiddler who played more enchanting music than the rest. The Chamberlain signaled him when the dance began and he stood forward and played a music so bewitching that no one could remember anything but the dance. The King's son danced with Buttercup and with Berry-bright and he smiled so kindly upon them that each though she surely would be asked to distribute the citrons and pomegranates that were on the table.

But the music ceased and nothing was heard but the jingle of the little silver bells that were hung across the Gallery. The fiddlers had left down fiddle and bow; all the maidens and all the Peers of the Realm were looking toward the entrance of the Solar Gallery. The King's son looked, and the heart in his breast gave a leap when he saw that she had come.

It was she indeed, the Matchless Maiden. All in silver was she dressed, with a shimmering veil and glimmering shoes. Her dark hair fell below her shoulders and her eyes were full of light. Slender was she as the barely noticed moon in the sky.

She curtsied to the right to the King's son and she curtsied to the left to the Peers of the Realm. She stood as if she were listening in delight to the chiming of the little silver bells that were hung across the gallery.

The King's son went to her, and after he had bowed, he said:

"Where have you come from, bright damsel?"

"From Lost-ember Moor," said she.

"And will you dance with me?" said he.

"When you rede aright where I've come from," said she.

The King's son drew back from her, not knowing what to say. Then the Duke who had the largest diamond in his shoe came forward and led her into the dance.

Dance after dance went on, and one Duke after the other asked the Matchless Maiden to be his partner. But when there was a lull in the music the King's son went to her and said:

"We beg of you to come to the table and distribute the citrons and pomegranates amongst the company."

The Matchless Maiden walked with him to

the table, and those who were little looked over the others' shoulders to watch her pass. She took a citron in one hand and a pomegranate in the other, and gracefully and graciously she offered them to one of the maidens.

The King's son went to the gallery where the musicians were. Besides the fiddler who played enchanting music there was a harper there who played music still more enchanting. The King's son spoke to him, and he took up his silver harp and began to play.

The music he played was so enchanting that it seemed to all who were there that they lived only in his notes. They forgot what was before and what was behind them. The King's son was the most enchanted of all; he stood still and watched the Matchless Maiden, the citrons and pomegranates in her hands, giving them gracefully and graciously to this one and that one of the company.

Suddenly there came a loud and a heavy sound into the gallery. It was the Clock in the Tower striking twelve. No one heeded the strokes, and the Matchless Maiden, filled with that enchanting music, went on giving the citrons and pomegranates to this one and that one in the company. But suddenly she stopped and listened to the last strokes of the Clock. The citrons and pomegranates fell from her hands and went rolling across the floor. She ran to the wide doorway. Before anyone knew she was out of the Gallery she was past the seven servitors and down the scarlet stairway. They saw her in the hall. But when the King's son with the Peers of the Realm, the fiddlers and the harper, and the score of servants who had lighted the candles came into the hallway, the maiden in the silver dress, with the shimmering veil and the glimmering shoes, was nowhere to be seen.

But now there was no one in the Castle that wasn't concerned about her. Even the outlandish servants in the underground kitchens heard of the stranger-maiden who had made an appearance at the two balls in the Solar Gallery, and they and the Ratcatcher talked for the length of a morning about her, forgetting the quarrel that they always had about the fewness of the rats taken, and the great quantity of tallow that was made away with.

The King's son called on the Chamberlain

seven times in the course of the morning. And each
time he informed him that if he did not do something to hold the Matchless Maiden after the
Clock struck twelve, he, the King's son, would have
him sent out of the Kingdom when he came to the
throne. The Chamberlain was all flurried and flus-
tered. He went to this one and that one, asking
what was to be done; no one could help him, and
we verily believe he would have been driven to distraction if it hadn't happened that he met the
King's Fool on the grand stairway. "How, in the
name of all the King's horses, can we hold the
Matchless Maiden who runs down this stairway
when the Clock strikes twelve?" he asked the Fool.
And the Fool put his hand to his mouth and whispered. . . . But what it was the Fool whispered will
have to be told you later.

Anyway the Chamberlain ran lightly down
the stairs and sprang lightly up the stairs. He had
the thousand candles lighted in the Solar Gallery.
He had the seven servitors take their places on the
grand stairway, with the silver candlesticks of
seven branches in their hands. Then the maidens
came up the stairway, the little bright earrings

96

gleaming in their ears. Buttercup and Berry-bright came in after all had assembled, so that they might have the opportunity of curtsying to the right to the King's son and to the left to the Peers of the Realm, with all the airs their mother had shown them.

The little silver bells strung across the Gallery chimed in the breeze; the nine nightingales began to sing in their darkened cages, and the Peers of the Realm and the maidens assembled indulged in most delightful conversation. Not so the King's son. He went from place to place and from company to company. It was on account of his restlessness that the dancing did not begin.

And even when the fiddlers tuned up their instruments and played the dancing tune, and when he was out on the floor with the partner he had chosen, the King's son was ever and always looking over his shoulder to the wide doorway that was the entrance of the Solar Gallery. Others, we must think, were looking toward that entrance too. For, as if it were at a signal, the music stopped and the dancing, and all the company, the maidens and the Dukes they were dancing with, all stood gathered together as the Matchless Maiden came in.

The King's son saw her standing there in a dress of gold, with a shining veil and golden shoes. She walked more gracefully than the others danced, a smile of gentleness was on her lips and the star on her forehead was plain to be seen.

The King's son went to her.

"Where have you come from, brightest of maidens?" said he.

"From where a dog's tongue lapped water from my hands," said she.

"I cannot rede where that may be, but will you not dance with me?"

"I may not dance with you till you rede all I say," said she.

He drew away from her, and the best favored of the young Dukes came, and, bowing before her, claimed her for a dance. When the dance was over and when the music was still, the King's son went to her and begged her to distribute amongst the company the citrons and pomegranates that were on the table. All the company stood in a double line to watch her pass; Buttercup and Berry-bright were standing opposite each other, and the bright little earrings fell out of their ears with the anger that came over them.

The Matchless Maiden took a citron in one hand and a pomegranate in the other and gracefully and graciously she handed them to Berrybright. And again she took a citron and a pomegranate and gracefully and graciously she handed them to Buttercup. To no others in the company did she hand citrons and pomegranates. Suddenly a loud and a heavy sound was heard in the Gallery. It was the Clock in the Tower striking twelve. The citrons and the pomegranates that were in her hands fell and rolled upon the floor.

She sped toward the wide doorway. Past the musicians and toward the grand stairway the Matchless Maiden ran. One, two, three, four, five, six, seven steps of the scarlet stairway she ran down. And then something held her foot.

It was the pitch that held her, the pitch that the Chamberlain had put there immediately she had entered the ballroom. That was what the Fool had whispered him to do when he met him on the grand stairway the time he was near distraction.

The pitch held her foot. The last strokes of the Clock were being struck. The company were running out of the ballroom. The Matchless Maiden took her foot out of her golden shoe and went speeding down the rest of the stairway.

The last of the seven servitors saw her in the hall. But when the King's son with the fiddlers and the servants and all the young Peers of the Realm came down into the hallway the maiden in the dress of gold, with the shining veil and the one golden shoe, was not to be seen. But the Chamberlain was there, standing before the King's son, with a golden shoe in his hands.

THE WISEST WOMAN COMES TO THE KING'S CASTLE

15   HAVING THE SHOE WAS NOT THE SAME AS having the shoe-wearer: they searched and searched everywhere for the maiden with the dress of gold, with the shining veil and the one golden shoe, but not a trace of her could they find. The Chamberlain went to search on his own account: into every dwelling around, hall or cabin, he went, asking every maiden that might be there to fit the shoe to her foot. They were all glad to try, but on none would the golden shoe go; it was too small for the foot of every grown maiden.

When the Chamberlain came back to the Castle the King's son made a declaration that he would wed only the maiden whose foot the golden shoe fitted. Then the maidens who were still in the castle sat ring-around on the lawn with their little shapely feet bare. But not to the foot of any of them could the Chamberlain fit the shoe of the Matchless Maiden.

Their mother had given Berry-bright and Buttercup a salve to rub on their feet so that the shoe might be helped to fit. Buttercup rubbed on the salve: as she did her heel shrunk away; then with great pain and difficulty she got the shoe to go on. She stood up to walk to where the King's son was standing but the pain in her foot was so afflicting that she had to sit down and cry to have the shoe taken off. Berry-bright rubbed on the salve and her great toe shrunk away. With great pain and difficulty she put on the golden shoe. She stood up to walk to where the King's son was standing; but the pain in her foot was so great that she too had to sit down and cry to have the shoe taken off. And the end of it all was that Berry-bright and Buttercup had to go limping to their mother.

What now was to be done to find the maiden

whose foot the golden shoe fitted? This one and that one advised this and that thing. But the ancient foster mother of the King's son went straight to the King himself, and this is what she said to him:

"Listen to the words of your gossip, King Daniel: only a woman's wit can help your son to find the Matchless Maiden that his heart is set upon winning. My own wits are not as sharp as they used to be or else I myself would help him. Now my advice to you is that you make proclamation asking to come to the Castle the woman who is the wisest in these parts. And that you may know she is the wisest she will have to come in this way: not naked yet with no clothes on, not fed and yet not fasting, in no one's company yet not alone. The woman who can come in this way will be the wisest in these parts, and she, you may be sure, will help your son to find the maiden whose foot the golden shoe will fit."

The King took his gossip's advice: he made a proclamation asking that she come to the Castle, the woman who was the wisest in those parts. And that he might know she was the wisest she was to come, not naked but with no clothes on, not fed and yet not fasting, in no one's company and yet not alone.

In the Castle and all around it every one talked of the King's proclamation. The Ratcatcher got so excited talking to the outlandish servants about it that he let the brown rats, the three biggest he had ever caught, bounce out of the cage and go running over Maid-alone who that minute was filling up her tub with the ashes of the third hearth.

The next day when he was walking in his private garden with his Councilors beside him a messenger came to the King to say that one was coming to see him in obedience to the proclamation he had caused to be made. The King sent for his son and for the Chamberlain and he told the messenger that whoever was coming in obedience to his proclamation should be brought into his private garden. His son came with the Chamberlain and with all the bright-haired and brown-haired and dark-haired maidens who still stayed in the King's Castle.

The maidens whispered, "How can she come so as to be not naked and yet with no clothes on, not fed and yet not fasting, not in company and yet

not alone?" And the Councilors said to one another, "What a great age she must be, this woman
who is the wisest in these parts!"

And then she came into the Garden. Not old
at all was she, but young and slender. She was not
naked and yet she had no clothes on, she was not
fed and yet she was not fasting, she was in no one's
company and yet she was not alone.

All round her body a dark and heavy fish net
was wrapped, she had a little apple between her
teeth the juice of which broke her fast and on her
shoulders there were two starlings that saved her
from being alone. The King looked her over and
over. "Maiden," he said, "as young as you are, I
find that you are the wisest woman in these parts."

The King's son took three steps to her and
stopped; took three more steps to her and stopped.
And all the time he looked at her like a man who
was falling into or wakening out of a trance.

"Can you help us to find the maiden whose
foot this shoe will fit?" said the Chamberlain. He
always carried the shoe about with him and now he
held it in his hand.

"It may be that I can, lord" said she. She held

her own bare foot as if she wanted him to fit the shoe on it.

But now a whisper was going round that this was the cinder-wench from the underground kitchens. "To think that she should imagine that the golden shoe that was tried on many a princess would go on her foot," some of the maidens were saying. The Chamberlain did not heed. He was now so used to fitting the golden shoe to a foot that was held for it that he went down on his knees and brought Maid-alone's foot to the shoe.

Easily the foot fitted the shoe; easily the Chamberlain buckled it on. And there stood Maid-alone with one white bare foot and one golden-covered foot standing in the grass of the King's garden, while the two starlings on her shoulders sang aloud.

"By all the King's horses," said the Chamberlain, "this is no other than the Matchless Maiden!"

"No other than the Matchless Maiden!" they all said.

The King's son took three more steps to her, and now it looked as if he were awakening out of a trance.

"Will the King give me permission to leave, so that I may put proper clothing on myself?" said Maid-alone.

"By all means we will give you permission if you say you will come back to us," said the King.

"I will come back," said Maid-alone.

Then, holding the golden shoe in her hand, Maid-alone ran through the grass of the King's garden and out through the gate. The maidens talked to each other, the King talked to his Councilors and the Councilors talked to the King, and the Chamberlain talked to everyone. But the King's son stood silent and apart, watching the gate that Maid-alone had gone through.

When they saw her again she had on a gleaming dress, with a glittering veil and gleaming shoes. The King himself rose from his seat in delight at her appearance. The King's son went to her. But all she said to him was, "You can rede now where I have come from: from Ditchland which is by Old Shoe Garden."

Again she got the King's permission to leave, and again she ran through the grass and out of the gate of the King's garden. They all talked and talked of her, saying that the King's son should be happy now that he had found indeed the Matchless Maiden. But the King's son stood leaning against a tree, with the red of shame coming and going in his face. He was thinking of the maiden who gathered berries in an old shoe for him, and how he rode his jennet against her while her mouth trembled and her eyes looked steadily on him.

All watched the gate for the Matchless Maiden's return. She came in a dress of silver, with a shimmering veil and glimmering shoes. The King himself took a step toward her, and all the Councilors began to say how dark her hair was, and how full of light were her eyes.

The King's son went to her, but all she said to him was, "You can rede where I have come from: from Last-ember Moor."

She got permission to go from the garden once more. She went, and all went to the gate that they might be quick to welcome her coming back. But the King's son stood on shame-fast feet: he thought of the time when he had let her go from the fire she had made into the darkness of the moor.

She came again into the King's garden. All in gold was she now, with a shining veil, and two golden shoes on her feet. The King himself took her hands, and the maidens who were there praised her for the star she had on her forehead.

But the King's son stood before her with head held down. "You can rede now where I've come from," she said to him, "from where a dog's tongue lapped water from my hands."

Again she asked permission to leave the garden. "But she is so lovely that we want to do nothing else but look on her," said the King. "But, please your Majesty," said the Chamberlain, "no one has seen the Matchless Maiden with her jewels on."

"No one has seen her with her jewels on," said the maidens.

The King gave her permission, and she went out of the garden, leaving all high in impatience for her return.

The King's son stood shame-fast, thinking of the time when he rode his high-mettled horse with his bell-mouthed hound beside him; she had come to him, bringing water for him in her hands. And he had not praised her hands, but had turned her away, bidding her bring water in her hands for his hound to lap his tongue in.

They watched and watched for the Matchless Maiden's return. They would take her into the King's castle, and give a feast for her and bestow gifts on her. But though they watched long and long she did not return. The Chamberlain went out to search for her. He went to this place and that place, and even down to the underground kitchens, but sign or token of Maid-alone who had come to be called the Matchless Maiden he did not find.

THE *CLOCK STRIKES* AND *MAID-ALONE* STAYS

16 ✿ DAYS THAT MADE A YEAR WENT BY; THE maidens went away from the Castle, and Dame Dale married her two limping daughters, Berry-bright and Buttercup, to the kennelmaster and the stablemaster. But still the King's son went searching for the Matchless Maiden.

He made many journeys and he brought certain quests to an end; but no Maid-alone did he find at the end of the quest or the end of the journey. Often the falconers saw him standing at the edge of the marsh, where, her bare feet in the marsh water, he had seen Maid-alone with the white and gray goose flock around her.

It was his Muime who told him about the two starlings that used to fly beside him when he rode abroad and come back with him from his journeys. They had their shelter beside her dormer window, and that is how she had come to notice them. Well, the next time he rode out he watched for the starlings and he followed where they flew. Down winding laneways they brought him where only elder bushes and briers grew. On he rode after them till he came to a small black house deep-sunken in the ground.

He went to the door and looked into the house. There, sitting by the fire and spinning gray threads on an old spindle he saw a woman in a Cloak of Crow-feathers. He left his horse standing and stepped into the house. The Old Woman looked at him and said, "Tell me what you have come to seek."

"The maiden who once wore the cloak you wear," said he.

"Where did that maiden come to you from?" said she.

"She came from Ditchland, by Old Shoe Garden," said he, "and from Last-ember Moor and from where a dog lapped water out of her hands."

"And have you betaken yourself to all these places?" said the Old Woman in the Cloak of Crowfeathers.

"I have. Many days did I spend at Ditchland searching for the shoe that was thrown down there. I found it. And on Last-ember Moor I spent days looking for the pot that was brought there. I fought with a Giant and did not come off scatheless. But I found and I have the pot. Then I sat by the well from which one brought water for a dog to lap his tongue in. Many days I was there, and I brought water to all the dogs that went past."

The Woman of a Thousand Years rose up and brought the King's son to the garden that was behind her little house. And there he saw Maid-alone standing in a little stream and gathering cresses.

Not the bronze dress, nor the silver dress nor the gold dress had she on now. She was dressed in brown wincey and her feet were bare. But more than ever in the King's son's eyes did she look the Matchless Maiden.

Just as he laid his eyes on her one burst through the hedge and came to her. It was the Chamberlain from the Castle. He cried out, "I have found you at last. Come with me to the King's Castle and to one who is dying for love of you."

She said, "Who is there that remembers me?"

"I, I, I,!" cried the King's son.

Maid-alone came again to the King's Castle: she looked on its stables and its kennels; its mews for the hawks and its meres for the herons; its ponds for the swans and parades for the peacocks; she looked on the little door that the third under-stewardess had opened to her on the morning she first came. By that little door she entered now. She went softly past the scullery where she used to eat her meal of scraps before she was banished to the ashy hearths, and she went past the Ratcatcher who was standing by his cage of brown rats, telling the outlandish servants that tallow was the one thing in the Castle that rats would not eat. She came to where the crooked passages and the winding stair-ways led up to the main hallway. Before her was the great, sweeping scarlet staircase. All alone she went up it, and there were no servitors standing there in their velvets, with branched silver candlesticks in their hands. And all alone she entered the Solar Gallery, and she found a cushioned seat before a fire of peat, and she sat down on it.

And into the Solar Gallery, closing the door behind him, came another. It was the King's son. Citrons and pomegranates were on the table, and he brought them to her, taking a place on a cushioned seat beside her. Then into the gallery came a loud and a heavy sound. It was the Clock in the Tower striking twelve. Maid-alone let the citrons and the pomegranates fall. But they did not roll far. Nor did she stand up to run away, for she remembered that she and the King's son were wed, and that two starlings had sung at their wedding and that they had leave to be together even though the clock struck twelve.